TEENAGE MUTANT NINJA TURTLES™

MEET LEATHERHEAD

adapted by Wendy Wax

based on the original teleplay

"What a Croc!" by Ben Townsend

illustrated by Patrick Spaziante

Simon Spotlight

New York   London   Toronto   Sydney

Visit us at abdopublishing.com

Spotlight Library bound edition © 2007. Spotlight is a division of ABDO Publishing Company, Edina, Minnesota.

From *Meet Leatherhead*. Text by Wendy Wax, based on the original teleplay "What a Croc!" by Ben Townsend. Illustrations by Patrick Spaziante. Based on the TV series *Teenage Mutant Ninja Turtles*™ as seen on Fox and Cartoon Network® Reprinted with permission of Simon Spotlight, Simon & Schuster Children's Publishing Division. All rights reserved.

Simon Spotlight

An Imprint of Simon & Schuster Children's Publishing Division
1230 Avenue of the Americas, New York, New York 10020

ISBN-13 978-1-59961-249-2 (reinforced library bound edition)
ISBN-10 1-59961-249-6 (reinforced library bound edition)

Library of Congress Cataloging-In-Publication Data
This book was previously cataloged with the following information:
  Wax, Wendy
    Meet Leatherhead / adapted by Wendy Wax ; based on the original teleplay "What a Croc!" by Ben Townsend ; illustrated by Patrick Spaziante.
      p. cm. -- (Teenage Mutant Ninja Turtles)
  ISBN 0-689-87711-0
    Summary: The Turtles get a big surprise when they meet Leatherhead, a mutated crocodile who was accidentally exposed to the Utrom's green ooze. As the Turtles listen to Leatherhead's story, they get another surprise when an old enemy emerges from the shadows.
    [1. Heroes--Fiction. 2. Martial arts--Fiction. 3. Turtles--Fiction.] I. Spaziante, Patrick, ill. II. Title. III. Series: Teenage Mutant Ninja Turtles ; #8.

[E]--dc22

2005296381

Michelangelo stared into the dark pool that led to the sewers. "I wish I were in my room reading comic books," he said.

"But I need your help, Mikey," said Donatello, holding up a steel pipe. "I need you to secure this pipe into the underwater entryway, so it won't close up when we cruise through in a submersible."

"Got it!" said Michelangelo. He grabbed the pipe and jumped in.

Michelangelo swam down to the entryway and put the steel pipe in place. Then he froze with fear! There in front of him was a large, crocodile-like creature. It had human arms and legs, razor-sharp teeth, and a green, spiked tail. The croc roared!

Get a grip, Michelangelo told himself. Splinter would tell
me to relax and fade into the background. As soon as the croc
turned away, Michelangelo quickly swam to the surface.

Michelangelo found all three of his brothers waiting for him. "You'll . . . never . . . believe . . . what I saw!" he said breathlessly. "It was part crocodile . . . part human!"

"I think Mikey's lost it!" said Raphael.

"It *really* exists!" insisted Michelangelo. "Come see for yourselves."

When the other Turtles refused to go, Donatello gave Michelangelo a scuba mask with a two-way radio and an underwater propulsion device. "The camera and transmitter will let us see your 'mystery croc' on our plasma screen . . . *if* it exists," he explained.

"Stay tuned, guys," said Michelangelo. "Mikey TV is taking you on a croc hunt!"

While underwater, Michelangelo saw the croc
near the entryway with a mechanical part in its mouth.

"I take it back, Mikey," Raphael said into the radio. "You're not insane."

"The chase is on!" said Michelangelo. He followed the croc to a place that looked *very* familiar. "Guys," he said, "you're never going to believe where I am!"

"Mikey's in our old lair!" said Donatello, staring at the plasma screen. "Big, dark, and scaly is living in our old home."

They watched as the croc stood on two legs and put on a lab coat and glasses.

"It's a big crocodile version of Don!" said Leonardo. "Look at his workshop!"

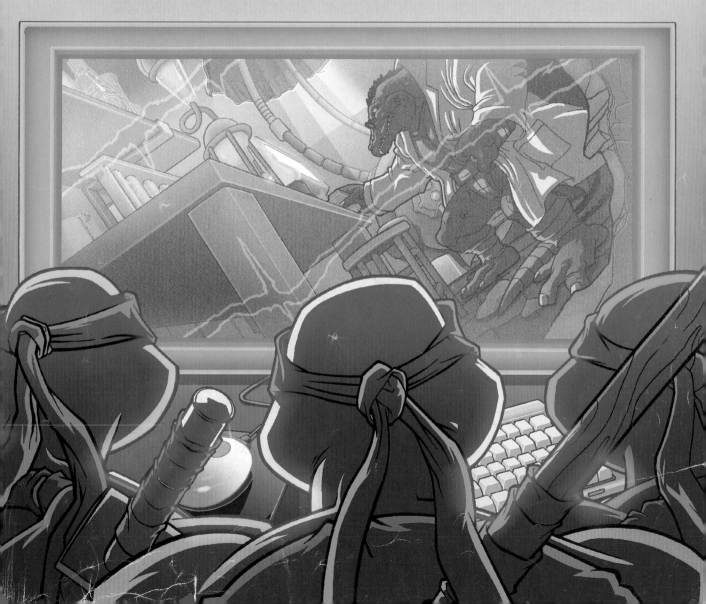

"I got the part!" the croc said to someone in the shadows. Then he attached the mechanical part to the back of an exoskeleton—which began to move. "That exoskeleton must be an Utrom!" Michelangelo said—much too loudly.

The croc spun around and saw Michelangelo. "An intruder!" he roared.

"N-nice crocodile . . . ," said Michelangelo, backing out of the lair. The croc charged at him, and for a while they struggled. Then the croc bit the propulsion device off Michelangelo's back, flung him several feet, and whacked him with its tail.

"Mikey! Mikey!" cried Raphael. But there was no answer.

While Michelangelo prepared to use his nunchaku, the croc became more human again. "I . . . I . . . am sorry," he said. "I got carried away."

Just then the Sewer Slider arrived. The Turtles jumped out, ready for action.

"It's okay, guys," said Michelangelo. "Croc and I are calling a truce."

The croc invited the Turtles into their old lair. "I am Leatherhead," he said.

"You're building a Transmat?" asked Donatello, admiring the work-in-progress.

"If you know about the Transmat, you must know about my family—the Utroms," said Leatherhead. Then he told his story.

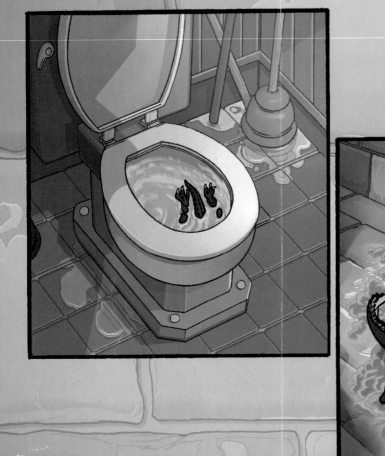

"I was once a pet that was thrown into the sewer," said Leatherhead. "The Utroms brought me to their home, where I was accidentally exposed to a mutagen. It affected my body and made me highly intelligent. The Utroms barely escaped when humans tried to destroy them. Once I finish building this Transmat, I'll finally be able to join my family again."

Just then an exoskeleton appeared in the doorway. The Turtles couldn't believe their eyes! Inside the exoskeleton's chest cavity was a jar that contained Baxter Stockman's head. "Don't trust those Turtles!" Stockman shouted. "They betrayed the Utroms!"

"He's a liar!" said Michelangelo. Leatherhead didn't know who to believe.

"It's time to put our anti-Turtle device to work!" said Stockman. He tossed some shapes into the air. They split apart, expanded, and joined together to form a Turtlebot!

"This doesn't look good," said Donatello. He spun his bo staff and stepped toward the Turtlebot. But the Turtlebot knocked him off his feet.

Michelangelo swung his nunchaku, but the Turtlebot blocked it again and again.

"The Turtlebot knows what we're going to do before we do it," said Donatello.

Using his staff, Donatello charged into the Turtlebot. It collapsed.

Stockman furiously slammed the Turtles—two at a time—to the floor.

"I've wanted my revenge ever since I worked for Shredder," said Stockman.

"You worked for Shredder?" Leatherhead asked, becoming angry. "You were never going to help me with the Transmat. Shredder was the Utroms' worst enemy!"

Stockman hurled a gas cylinder that burst into flames when it hit the ceiling of the lair. *Boom!*

"Let's go, Leatherhead!" said Michelangelo. "The ceiling is collapsing!"
But before Leatherhead could move, the ceiling beams fell, trapping him.
"Go, my friend," said Leatherhead, with tears running down his snout.
The Turtles managed to escape—just in time!

"Poor Leatherhead," Michelangelo said sadly. "He was so alone."
"I wish we could have saved him," added Leonardo.
"Things sure get rough at times," said Donatello. "But at least we have each other."